FIX-IT DUCK

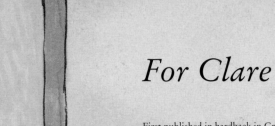

For Clare

First published in hardback in Great Britain by HarperCollins Children's Books in 2001
First published in paperback by Collins Picture Books in 2002
This edition published in 2009 by HarperCollins Children's Books

10 9 8 7 6 5

ISBN: 978-0-00-730289-5

Collins Picture Books is an imprint of the Children's Division, part of HarperCollins Publishers Ltd.
HarperCollins Children's Books is a division of HarperCollins Publishers Ltd.

Text and illustrations copyright © Jez Alborough 2001

Visit our website at: www.harpercollins.co.uk

Printed and bound in China

Jez Alborough
FIX-IT DUCK

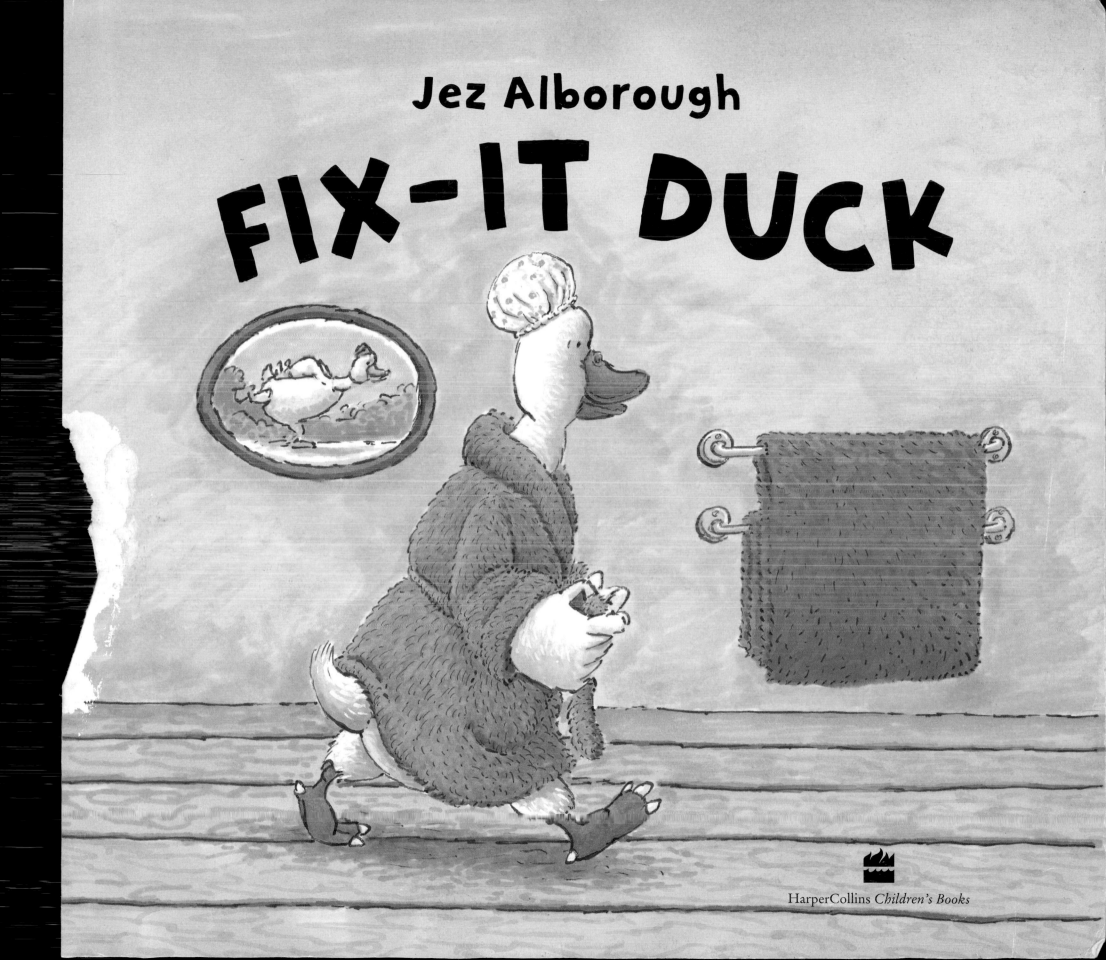

HarperCollins *Children's Books*

Plop! goes the drip that drops in the cup.
Duck looks down and Duck looks up.

'A leak in the roof.
Oh, what bad luck!

This is a job for…

FIX-IT DUCK.'

He says, 'It's easy to repair.'
But how's he going to reach up there?

He can't climb up –
it's much too steep.

So he drives round to borrow

a ladder from Sheep.

Over the puddles   to Sheep's little house,

he hops and he skips   then, OOPS, he trips!

'Sheep!' calls Duck.
'It's only me.'

And he explains how the rain
had dripped in his tea.

When he reaches the part about fixing the leak,
they hear a rattle, creak and a squeak.

'It's my window,' says Sheep,
'it won't close, it's stuck.'

'This is a job for
FIX-IT DUCK.'

He does what he can to close up the gap.
He glues it, screws it and gives it a tap.

'The problem,' says Duck, 'is your glass is too thin.'
'My house,' wails Sheep. 'The rain's coming in!'

'What we need,' says Duck, with a glint in his eye,
'is to pull your house to somewhere dry.

Goat's got a shed. It can shelter inside.
Let's hook up your jeep and go for a ride.

Drive back slowly,
'til I say stop.'

Then all of a sudden,
something goes POP!

'A puncture,' says Duck. 'More bad luck.
We'll have to use my pick-up truck.'

But Sheep's little house won't join to the truck.

'This is a job for…   FIX-IT DUCK.'

'We're off,' says Duck as they speed down the track.

'Slow down on the bends,'
calls Sheep from the back.

'Turn left,' he bleats as they skid round a curve.
'Hold tight,' comes the quack as the truck starts to swerve.

And the house should follow behind but instead...

...it unhooks from the truck

and rolls on straight ahead.

When Duck gets to Goat's he starts to explain
why they'd brought Sheep's house which was letting in rain.

'But where is it?' asks Goat.
Then as Duck turns to see,

Frog runs up shouting,
'It's following me!'

'Look up on the hill,'
gasps Goat in dismay.

'It's Sheep,' quacks Duck,
'and he's coming this way!'

'*Run!*' cries Frog.
'He's going to crash!'

'H-E-L-P!' bleats Sheep.

'It's broken,' says Duck. 'What a lot of bad luck.'

'Oh no!' moans Sheep, 'not...

FIX-IT

If only he hadn't come calling on me.
If only that rain hadn't dripped in his tea.'

DUCK!

'Not rain,' says Frog, with a shy little cough.

'He forgot to turn his bath tap off.'

WATCH OUT, here comes DUCK!

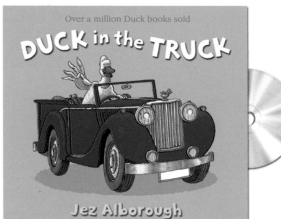

HB ISBN: 978-0-00-198346-5 £10.99
PB ISBN: 978-0-00-730262-8 £5.99
PB & CD ISBN: 978-0-00-731541-3 £7.99

KATE GREENAWAY MEDAL
HIGHLY COMMENDED
PB ISBN: 978-0-00-730289-5 £6.99
PB & CD ISBN: 978-0-00-724209-2 £7.99

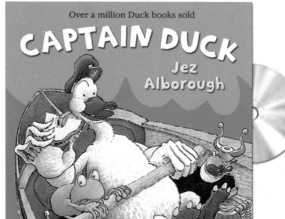

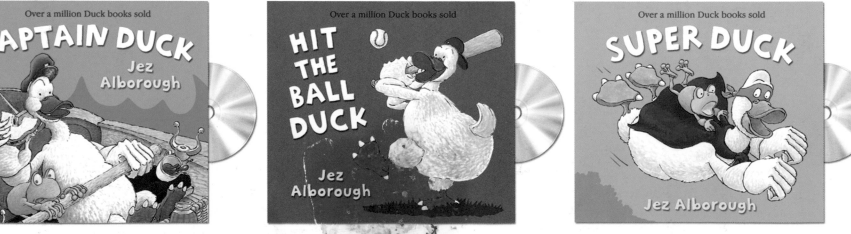

PB ISBN: 978-0-00-730290-1 £6.99
PB & CD ISBN: 978-0-00-721421-1 £7.99

PB ISBN: 978-0-00-730291-8 £6.99
PB & CD ISBN: 978-0-00-721219-4 £7.99

PB ISBN: 978-0-00-727327-0 £5.99
PB & CD ISBN: 978-0-00-731547-5 £7.99

Collect all the hilarious books in the series!

PB ISBN. 978-0-00-724356-3 £5.99

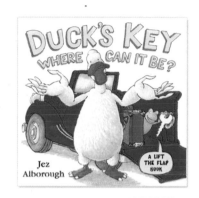

SHORTLISTED FOR THE
BOOKTRUST EARLY YEARS
PRE-SCHOOL AWARD
PB ISBN: 978-0-00-717765-3 £5.99

Board book ISBN:
978-0-00-714214-9 £4.99

Board book ISBN:
978-0-00-718279-4 £4.99

Board book ISBN:
978-0-00-720927-9 £5.99

Board book ISBN:
978-0-00-724357-0 £5.99

Jez Alborough was born and grew up in Kingston upon Thames. He graduated from art school in Norwich with a BA honours degree in Graphic Design. Since then, he has created more than thirty children's picture books. Jez's funny stories about Duck have sold more than one and half million copies worldwide, firmly establishing him as one of today's most talented author/illustrators. Jez lives with his wife in London.

To find out more about Duck visit: JezAlborough.com